SURVIVAL
Shipwreck!

Frieda Wishinsky

Cover by
Norman Lanting

Interior illustrations by
Don Kilby

Scholastic Canada Ltd.

Toronto New York London Auckland Sydney
Mexico City New Delhi Hong Kong Buenos Aires

Scholastic Canada Ltd.
604 King Street West, Toronto, Ontario M5V 1E1, Canada

Scholastic Inc.
557 Broadway, New York, NY 10012, USA

Scholastic Australia Pty Limited
PO Box 579, Gosford, NSW 2250, Australia

Scholastic New Zealand Limited
Private Bag 94407, Botany, Manukau 2163, New Zealand

Scholastic Children's Books
Euston House, 24 Eversholt Street, London NW1 1DB, UK

www.scholastic.ca

Library and Archives Canada Cataloguing in Publication
Wishinsky, Frieda, author
     Shipwreck! / Frieda Wishinsky.
(Survival)
Issued in print and electronic formats.
ISBN 978-1-4431-4641-8 (pbk.).--ISBN 978-1-4431-4642-5 (ebook).--
ISBN 978-1-4431-4643-2 (Apple edition)
     1. Empress of Ireland (Steamship)--Juvenile fiction. I. Title.
II. Series: Wishinsky, Frieda. Survival.
PS8595.I834S55 2015   jC813'.54   C2015-901890-0
                                        C2015-901891-9

6 5 4 3 2 1   Printed in Canada   121   15 16 17 18 19

For my friend Roselyne Kraft

CHAPTER ONE

May 29, 1914

As Albert peered over the ship's railing at the St. Lawrence River below, he heard someone coming. He turned around. It was Grace! What was she doing on deck so late?

Grace's long hair flew in the breeze. She looked like she'd jumped out of bed without even combing her hair.

"What are you doing here?" she asked Albert.

"I could ask you the same question," he replied.

"My father was snoring so loudly I couldn't sleep. What about you?"

"I couldn't sleep either. So I came out to see the stars."

Albert and Grace leaned against the railing and stared at the night sky and the river, calm as a bathtub. Then they heard a clang.

"Hey! Did you hear that?" Grace whispered. "Listen. There it goes again!"

"Look! There's a ship!" said Albert, pointing to a large black ship down the river. "I wonder what kind it is."

Soon a fog rolled in. It was so thick it was hard to see anything. They waited a few minutes for the fog to lift.

"This fog isn't letting up," said Albert, yawning. "And I'm getting really tired. I'm ready to head in."

Grace nodded. "Me, too."

As Grace and Albert made their way to their cabins, a blast from the ship's horn made them jump.

"What was *that*?" asked Grace.

"I don't know."

Suddenly the ship lurched sharply to the side

and cold water seeped in. Albert grabbed Grace's hand and began to run.

The *Empress of Ireland* was sinking!

CHAPTER TWO

May 28, 1914

"Ouch! Get off my foot." A skinny girl with long auburn hair and dark green eyes glared at Albert. A short navy blue jacket covered her white blouse. Her black shoes peeked through the hem of her long navy blue skirt.

"Sorry. I didn't see your foot." Albert tried moving forward, but the dock was packed and there was little room to manoeuvre.

"You're not a Mountie, are you?" The girl pointed to Albert's wide Stetson hat and the brass buttons sparkling on his stiff red jacket.

"No. I'm with the Salvation Army. I'm in the Youth Band." Albert lifted up his trumpet case to show her.

"I've seen the Salvation Army on the street, collecting money to help the poor. My friends call your army the Sally Ann. Is it true that everyone from the Salvation Army smiles all the time?"

"You mean like this?" Albert grinned so widely his mouth hurt.

The girl laughed. "Are you going to London?"

"Yes. I'm going to the Salvation Army's International Congress with my father, my uncle Thomas, my aunt Betsy and my cousin Lewis." Albert gestured toward his family.

Albert's father, uncle and cousin wore identical uniforms, but unlike Albert's, their hats fit perfectly.

"My name's Albert McBride," he told the girl, pushing his hat back on his head. He extended his hand, and his hat tipped over his eyebrows. Dark brown curls poked out underneath the sides.

The girl shook his hand firmly. "I'm Grace O'Riley," she said. She looked Albert up and down as if inspecting him for a parade. "Your hat is too big."

"I know. It always falls off. Father said he'd get me another one, but in the rush to organize the trip, he forgot."

Grace laughed. Her eyes twinkled like emeralds. "Is the band going to give a concert on the ship?"

"Yes, the Staff Band will. I wish I could play with them, but I'm only in the Youth Band. You should come and hear them."

"I will. I like music." Grace looked up at the ship. "Isn't she beautiful?" she asked.

Albert peered up. The giant ship loomed over the dock like a floating castle. Large, white lifeboats hung off the top deck. A red-and-white-checkered flag flew in the breeze. Steam winches hauled boxes, trunks and suitcases for storage in the hold deep below.

The first-class passengers were already boarding. Many of them had attendants to carry their belongings. Their luggage, marked WANTED, accompanied them aboard.

"I can't wait to sail on the ocean. I've never sailed before," said Albert.

"I've sailed with my father back in Toronto. But that was on Lake Ontario. This is my first time on a giant ship on the Atlantic. This is going to be a wonderful adventure," said Grace.

The ship's whistle blew. The engines hummed, and smoke curled up to the sky. People gathered below the ocean liner, ready to wave goodbye to friends and relatives.

"We'll be boarding at any moment!" said Grace, clapping her hands.

Albert tucked his trumpet close to his chest. As he did, his hat fell forward and hit his nose. He straightened his hat and stood taller to keep it from falling again.

"Come on!" said Grace. "The line is moving."

Albert picked up his battered black leather suitcase and began to move forward with the crowd.

"Ouch! There you go again, mashing my toes," groaned Grace.

"I'm sorry. It's just . . ."

"I know. It's crowded here. But if we're going to be friends, Albert McBride, you have to promise to watch where you're stepping."

"I promise," said Albert, as the new friends headed toward the gangplank of the *Empress of Ireland*.

CHAPTER THREE

"Can you take over for Lewis?" asked Albert's father as soon as Albert entered the cabin.

Albert stared at his father. "Me?"

"Lewis isn't feeling well. The bandmaster wants you to play in Lewis's place. It's a great honour, son."

Albert had always wanted to play with the Staff Band, but he never thought he'd have a chance so soon. Could he do it? He knew all the songs they played, so why was his heart pounding? Albert took a deep breath. "Okay," he told his father.

"Good. Make me proud, son." His father shook his hand.

"I'll try my best, Father."

"Let's go."

Albert followed his father out of the cabin, down the hall and up to the Promenade deck. His stomach knotted as he stood beside his father and uncle. He wanted to play well.

A large group of passengers had gathered to hear them. Albert looked out at the crowd. Grace was in the front row, smiling at him. She waved as the bandmaster gave the signal to begin.

Albert lifted his trumpet to his mouth. The crowd broke into loud applause as soon as the first notes rang out. Many knew the song — "O Canada." Some, including Grace, sang along. To Albert's relief, he hit all the right notes.

After "O Canada," the band played another familiar song: "Auld Lang Syne." The audience burst into applause again. It wasn't New Year's, of course — the traditional time to sing it — and they weren't saying goodbye to the old year, but they were saying goodbye to Canada.

Albert had always liked the melody of "Auld Lang Syne," but he thought the words were strange. Why should anyone forget old friends and acquaintances just because it was a new year, or like now, because they were taking a trip? He didn't want to forget his friends, and he didn't want them to forget him. He already missed his best friend from school.

The *Empress* was ready to pull away from the Quebec City dock. The bandmaster signalled to begin the last song, a hymn. Albert lifted his trumpet again. Grace waved to him. Then she drew her lips up and made a funny face. Albert looked away so he wouldn't laugh. As he did, his hat slid down all the way to his nose. His face turned as red as his uniform. His fingers slipped off the keys and his trumpet squeaked. His father shot him a look. Albert quickly shoved his hat back into position. His hand shook as he picked up the song.

He didn't look at Grace this time. He didn't look
at anyone. He'd been so excited to play with the
band, and now he'd made a mistake. What would
his father say to him? Would the bandmaster ever
let him play with them again?

The audience sang along to the hymn. They sang

his mother's favourite line: "God be with you till we meet again." His mother had said those words when he hugged her goodbye a week earlier. "I'll miss you, Albert," she'd said, wiping away tears. "Promise me you'll be careful. Promise you'll take care of yourself."

"I will," promised Albert. "Don't worry, Mother. I'll be fine."

A loud whistle sounded from the ship, and everyone on the deck and waiting on the pier below cheered. The ship was sailing.

Albert and the band played the last notes of the hymn. The audience applauded loudly and warmly again. Albert wiped his trumpet as the ship made its way onto the St. Lawrence River. People on the pier waved handkerchiefs, flags and hats, bidding their friends and relatives goodbye.

They were on their way now.

As Albert straightened his hat again, someone tapped him on the shoulder.

It was Grace. "You *are* a good trumpet player, Albert McBride," she said, grinning at him. "I didn't mean to mess you up. But you got back to your song just like that!" Grace snapped her fingers.

"Thanks!" Albert smiled. He wished he hadn't made a mistake in front of all those people, but Grace was right — he'd kept playing.

Albert liked Grace, even if she did like to tease. He was happy to meet someone his age to share the six-day trip across the Atlantic.

CHAPTER FOUR

"Could you tell me which way to Cabin 7 in second class?" Albert asked a steward. Everyone in the band had returned to their cabins while he was speaking to Grace. Then Grace had dashed back to her cabin to meet her parents. Albert had wanted to look out at the river before heading back. Only now he was lost! The ship was huge, and he had no idea which way to go.

The steward smiled. "The *Empress* is confusing. I've been directing people to their cabins for the last hour."

"I wish I had a map of the ship," said Albert.

The steward pulled a piece of paper and a pencil from his pocket. "Here. I'll draw you a map and show you your cabin. That should help you find your way around."

"How many passengers are on board?" asked Albert as the steward drew the map.

"There are 1057 passengers aboard — 253 in second class. And there's our captain now — Captain Kendall."

Captain Kendall nodded to Albert and the steward as he surveyed the deck. Albert nodded back. Then he thanked the steward and headed to his cabin.

Albert's cabin was on the port side of the ship. He found his father there unpacking. Mr. McBride looked up when Albert walked in. "Oh, there you are! I saw you speaking to that young lady after the concert. I hope she enjoyed the music."

"She did. But I felt terrible when I hit that wrong note."

"That was unfortunate, son."

"Next time I won't make any mistakes. You'll see, Father."

Albert's father patted him on the back. "I hope so. Not everyone your age is given the opportunity to play with the regular band."

Albert sighed. He wanted to tell his father that it wasn't his fault he'd made a mistake, but his father hated excuses. "Just get the job done" was his motto. So Albert said nothing.

"Why don't you take the two bottom drawers of the dresser for your clothes," said his father.

Albert opened his suitcase and began to remove his belongings. Once he'd found a place for everything, he pulled a postcard from his suitcase. "I promised Mother and Eddie that I'd write them as soon as I arrived aboard the *Empress*," he said.

"They'll be glad to hear from you. Your mother worried about you joining me on this trip."

"I know," said Albert, remembering the conversation he had the night before he and his father left King City to catch the train in Toronto to Quebec City.

"Have a wonderful time, but don't wander off on your own. A big city like London can be dangerous," his mother had said.

"I'll be fine, Mother. Really, I will. Don't worry," Albert reassured her for the third time that day.

"Don't forget to walk across London Bridge," said Eddie. "And don't forget to visit the tower where all those prisoners were held before . . ." Eddie made a chopping motion with his hand. Swords, cannons, guns and gallows fascinated him.

Albert smiled, remembering the look on Eddie's face. Then he signed his name to the postcard and checked the watch his grandparents had given him for his twelfth birthday in March. There was still time before dinner to explore.

"I'm going out to mail this, Father. Then I want to look around the ship."

"Be careful. You don't know your way around yet, Albert. The *Empress* is big. It's easy to get lost."

Albert sighed. If only his parents didn't treat

him like a little kid. He wasn't going to get lost. He showed his father the map the steward had drawn for him. "I'll use this to find my way around," he said.

"Good. Don't forget dinner is promptly at seven." His father always reminded him to be punctual.

"I'll be back in time for dinner. I promise."

CHAPTER FIVE

"Hello again!"

Albert looked up. He was checking the address on his postcard when the door to a nearby cabin popped open. It was Grace!

"Hello," said Albert, grinning at her. "We keep bumping into each other. My father and I are in a cabin just down the hall from here."

"That makes us almost neighbours. Where are you going?"

"I want to mail this postcard to my mother and brother — and to look around the ship. How about you?"

"I was about to explore the ship, too. Do you want to explore together?"

"Sure, but I have to be back in time for dinner."

"Me, too. Come on. If we hurry we can see all of second class before then."

"Let's go this way," said Albert, pointing left.

As Albert and Grace raced down the hall they almost bumped into a steward holding a tray of tea, biscuits and cups.

"Sorry," said Albert.

"No harm done," said the steward. "You're the young man I drew the map for, aren't you?"

"Yes. I didn't get lost this time." Albert showed him the postcard. "Do you know where I can post this card?"

The steward took a look at the address. "King City. That's a little north of Toronto, isn't it? I have a cousin living on a farm there. Why don't you give me the postcard, and I'll deliver it to the mailroom for you. The *Lady Evelyn* will pick it up after midnight."

"Thanks. My mother and brother will be excited to receive this from the ship."

"Well, they should get your card even before we arrive in England." The steward tipped his hat to Grace and Albert.

Albert and Grace waved to the steward and headed for their first stop — the second-class smoking room. When they peeked in, Grace made a face and pinched her nose. "Ugh. I don't want to get any closer to *that* room. Those cigars stink."

Albert laughed. "Look! There's the music room. I bet it smells better in there and there's no one inside. Let's go in."

The music room had lots of plush chairs, polished wood tables and a grand piano.

"Can you play?" asked Grace.

"No. Can you?"

"I took a few lessons, but I'm not very good."

"Oh, come on. Don't be modest. Play something."

Grace ran her fingers along the keys. "The only piece I sort of remember is *'Für Elise.'*"

"I know that one. It's by Beethoven."

Albert pulled the bench from under the piano with a flourish. "For you, madam!"

Grace rolled her eyes as she sat down. "Thanks, but I warned you." She placed her hands on the keys, took a deep breath and began. She hit a jarring wrong note immediately. "See. I told you."

"I hit a wrong note today, too. Don't worry. Just start again," said Albert.

Grace placed her hands on the keys again. This time she played a few bars before she hit another wrong note. She threw her hands up. "I thought I'd remember the piece better. It's the only one I was good at, but I haven't played *'Für Elise'* in two years."

"Why did you stop playing?"

"I'm not musical. Even my teacher agreed. She said I didn't have a musical 'ear' and I didn't practise my scales enough. You're good at music."

"I wasn't very good today. You should have seen my father's face when I made that mistake."

"That wasn't your fault. I wish I could play like you. But I'm good at other things, like running and swimming."

Albert grinned. "Well, then, I'll race you to the second-class dining room." He showed Grace where it was located on his map. "One. Two. Three.

Go!" he said.

They ran through the corridors of the *Empress*. Huffing and puffing, they reached the second-class dining room at the same time. "Tie!" gasped Albert.

The waiters were starting to set up for dinner. Albert and Grace stared at the cozy booths along the walls, the fancy wood panelling and the long tables in the middle.

"Let's go up on the boat deck before we're shooed out of here," said Grace. "I want to get a look at the towns we pass along the St. Lawrence River. Once we're in the Atlantic we won't see land for days."

They dashed up to the boat deck. They leaned against the railing near the lifeboats, taking in the view and watching birds fly overhead. They peered at the small towns, the pine forests and the green fields lining the shores of the river.

"I wonder how cold the water is down there," said Albert, bending over the railing.

"Pretty cold. It hasn't warmed up enough since

winter. I love swimming, but not in icy water."

"How did you learn to swim?" asked Albert.

"My father taught me when I was little. He thinks everyone should know how to swim!"

"I only know how to dog paddle."

"Dog paddling can keep you afloat for a long time," said Grace.

"A lifeboat is better for staying afloat," said Albert, laughing.

"At least there are enough lifeboats for everyone on the *Empress*. My father said that after the *Titanic* sank two years ago, all ships had to have enough lifeboats for all the passengers. Hey! What time is it now?"

Albert looked at his watch. "It's almost dinner! I promised to be on time."

"I'd better get back, too. Let's look around some more tomorrow before breakfast."

❊　❊　❊

Albert's table was in the middle of the room and filled with people from the Salvation Army. Everyone was talking about the voyage across the Atlantic and planning which sights to see in London.

"Thanks for taking my place today, kid," Albert's cousin Lewis said as he sat down next to Albert. "The way I was feeling, I couldn't possibly have played with the band."

"How are you feeling now?" asked Albert.

"Much better. I never thought I'd get sick before we even set sail. Look! Here comes the bandmaster now."

Albert's heart pounded as the bandmaster approached their table. The bandmaster shook his father's and Lewis's hands and then patted Albert on the shoulder.

"Thanks for helping us out today, Albert. But I think you'd better get yourself a new hat."

Albert's face turned red. He knew the bandmaster was referring to his mistake.

"What's the matter, kid?" asked Lewis. "Are you

feeling sick, too? And what's that about your hat?"

"It's too big for me. That's all. I'm fine."

"Isn't that the young lady you were talking to earlier?" asked Albert's father, pointing to the door.

Albert looked up. Grace and her parents were heading for a table at the other side of the dining hall. Grace waved to Albert and mouthed "tomorrow." Albert nodded and waved back.

Lewis poked Albert in the ribs. "Is that your new *girl*friend, kid?"

"She's not my girlfriend. She's just a friend. And I'm not a kid." Lewis constantly joked that Albert was a kid even though, at eighteen, he was just barely an adult himself. "She reminded me that we agreed to meet early tomorrow to explore the ship."

Lewis jabbed him in the ribs again. "I was just *kid*ding, Albert. Good luck getting up early! Early's not for me. I'm sleeping in until right before breakfast."

CHAPTER SIX

Albert tossed back and forth in his bunk. He kept picturing the disappointment on his father's face as he hit the wrong note on his trumpet.

If only he hadn't looked at Grace. If only his hat fit better. If only . . .

It was no use. He checked his watch. It was almost one! Maybe it would help if he went out on deck. At home he loved sneaking out to see the stars at night. It always made him feel better when he had something on his mind.

Albert slipped out of his bunk and into his clothes. He grabbed a jacket and headed to the Promenade deck. It had been less than nine hours since the *Empress* set sail. The ship was still making its way along the St. Lawrence River toward the Atlantic.

Albert took a deep breath. He felt better already. He looked out across the river. The stars shimmered in the sky. Their sparkle reflected on the water. It was so peaceful. So beautiful. So . . .

What was that noise? It sounded like footsteps. Someone was heading toward him.

Albert turned around.

It was Grace! She looked like she'd jumped out of bed without even combing her hair.

"What are you doing here?" she asked.

"I could ask you the same question," he replied.

"My father was snoring so loudly I couldn't sleep. What about you?"

"I couldn't sleep either. So I came out to see the stars."

Grace looked out over the water. "It's beautiful out here."

"It feels like there's no one on board but us," said Albert.

Grace pointed to the deck above them. "And those crewmen on watch duty. I hope they don't shoo us back to bed."

"Shhh. They'll hear us."

"Sorry," whispered Grace. "Do you think we'll see any whales tonight? I've heard there are whales in the St. Lawrence."

"I don't think whales come out at night."

The two stood there quietly scanning the river and staring intently over the water. Then they heard a clang.

"Hey! Do you hear that?" Grace whispered. "Listen. There it goes again!"

"Look! There's a ship!" said Albert, pointing to a large black ship down the river. "I wonder what kind it is."

"It's not beautiful like the *Empress*. That's for sure."

"Maybe it's a ghost ship," said Albert.

"Or it could be a pirate ship, and pirates plan to board the *Empress* and steal our diamonds and jewels."

"Well, they won't get my new watch," said Albert, tapping his wrist.

"What time is it?"

Albert checked his watch. "Twenty minutes to two."

"Wow! I've never been up this late."

A light fog began to roll in. Albert and Grace lingered near the railing for a few more minutes hoping the fog would pass, but it only grew thicker.

"This fog isn't letting up." said Albert, yawning.

"And I'm getting really tired. I'm ready to head in."

Grace nodded. "Me, too."

As Grace and Albert made their way to their cabins, a blast from the ship's horn made them jump.

"What was *that*?" asked Grace.

"I don't know. Listen! There it goes again. One. Two. Three."

"Albert, something's wrong," said Grace.

Albert peered through a porthole. "I can see some lights. Maybe it's that big dark ship we saw before."

"Or—" The floor shook beneath them. "Did you feel that?"

"Yes! It felt like we hit something," said Albert. "But how could we hit something?"

Suddenly the ship listed hard and fast to starboard. Albert's eyes widened. His heart pounded as water began to seep into the ship.

Albert grabbed Grace's hand and raced down the hall. "We have to warn our families. The *Empress* is sinking!"

CHAPTER SEVEN

Albert and Grace rushed toward their cabins, struggling to keep their balance on the sloping floor.

Albert's heart pounded so hard he could hear it in his ears. Grace was breathing heavily. They leaned against the walls for support as they struggled to advance through the tilting corridors.

They were close to their cabins now.

People poured out of the neighbouring cabins.

"What's happening?" screamed a woman in a long flowered nightgown.

"What should I do?" yelled another woman holding a baby.

"My papers . . ." moaned a man.

A few people with lifebelts made their way

toward the top deck. Others stood around, dazed and confused.

"Hurry! Put on these lifebelts. Head for the lifeboats on the boat deck," yelled a steward. "Move quickly!" He banged on the cabin doors.

Albert and Grace each grabbed an armful of lifebelts from the steward and rushed to their cabins.

"Father! We have to get off the ship," screamed Albert, pounding on the door. "Father!"

Albert's father pried the door open. He rubbed his eyes. "What's happened, Albert?"

"The ship is sinking! We have to get up on deck. Put this on, quickly." Albert handed his father a lifebelt. "I'll check on the others."

Albert untied the strings of a lifebelt and slipped it on himself. Then he banged on the door of the next cabin, where the rest of his family had been asleep.

His uncle yanked the door open. "What's happening? Why is everyone screaming? Why—"

"The ship is sinking," Albert cried. "You have to get

out. Now!" Albert made his way into their cabin. He tossed lifebelts to his aunt, uncle and cousin. "There's no time left! Move. Please." His voice was desperate.

Aunt Betsy scrambled to find something to cover her nightgown. Lewis slipped a pair of pants over his pyjamas.

"Quick. Put your lifebelts on and get out," shouted Albert.

"You go on, Albert," said Uncle Thomas. "I'll help your aunt and Lewis. We'll find you later. Go on, lad. Go!"

Albert hugged his uncle and aunt and left. His father was in the hall in his lifebelt. Grace was there, too, with her parents. Her mother was shaking and sobbing.

"It will be all right, Mother," said Grace, tightening her mother's lifebelt. "We just have to hurry. Please. Follow me and Albert. We know the way."

Her mother's long brown hair hung loose and dishevelled. A black jacket was draped over her frilly pink nightgown. She shivered and clutched her handbag against her lifebelt. Grace's father's lifebelt was wrapped against his black robe. They followed Albert and Grace down the hall.

It was jammed. People screamed, cried, begged for help. Babies wailed. Toddlers called for their mothers. No one knew where to go or what to do.

"Let's go!" called Albert. "This way!" They wove through the crowded hall and struggled up the packed stairs.

"Follow me!" Albert shouted over the din of voices. The ship listed more and more with each step. The lights flickered as water gushed in from the portholes and through doorways. It rose up past their ankles. It was harder and harder to walk.

"Help!" cried Grace's mother, slipping in the icy water. Grace turned. She and her father pulled her mother up and out of the swirling water. Her mother's nightgown was drenched. Her hair was soaking wet. She sobbed.

Grace shivered. Her blouse was wet all the way through.

"This way!" shouted Albert.

They reached the top of the stairs. They kept going until they made it to the boat deck. It too was packed with people, who were clinging to the railings as the ship's starboard side leaned into the water.

"Look, Albert," shouted Grace. Her lips quivered as she pointed down. Bodies floated everywhere. The leg of a piano, mirrors, lamps, broken chairs and tabletops bobbed up and down beside the bodies. Those still alive clung to the debris.

The screams and cries of the injured pierced Albert like a knife.

And then the lights went out.

"Help!"

"Where are you, John?"

"What should I do?"

"We're going to drown. Help us! Please!"

People's screams and voices rose higher and higher as Albert, his father, Grace and her parents reached the spot where the lifeboats had hung hours before. In the darkness they could just make out dangling ropes.

"Where are the lifeboats?" shouted Grace.

"There! Look!" Albert said.

Two lifeboats lay below them, smashed to bits. Worse than that, the *Empress* was almost completely on her starboard side now. The giant ship was about to sink.

"We have to jump," said Albert. "It's our only chance."

"Hold on to that lifebelt. Cling to anything solid you can find," said his father. "I love you, Albert."

Albert gulped. "I love you."

"Dog paddle," said Grace. "I want to hear you play the trumpet again, Albert."

"Swim hard, Grace. You know how."

Albert looked at his friend. He looked at his father. Then he took a deep breath and jumped.

CHAPTER EIGHT

Down, down Albert sank. Darkness enveloped him. Cold, briny water filled his mouth, his nose, his ears. He couldn't breathe. He pumped up and down with his arms and legs till he rose to the surface. He floated. He spit out water and coughed.

Breathe. Breathe. You're alive!

Albert looked up. The ship's huge stacks leaned heavily toward the water. They were going to fall. When they did, everything and everyone close by would be sucked under along with the ship.

Albert paddled hard. He had to get away from the ship. His arms ached. His chest throbbed. But he kept paddling. Could he make it? Did he have the strength? Thank goodness he had his lifebelt.

Every part of him was cold. It felt like he was floating in a giant tub filled with ice. He couldn't feel his toes or his feet. His hands felt frozen, but he forced them to move, to paddle.

Paddle, he told himself. *Get away.*

His stomach churned. A sour taste rose to his throat and up to his mouth. He spit, but the sour taste remained.

Paddle. Paddle.

He searched for signs of his father, Grace or her parents. He looked for his aunt, uncle and Lewis. He couldn't see anything in the dark but bodies and slabs of jagged wood. A drum like the one the Salvation Army band played bobbed in the water. A man clung to a desk, moaning.

A long table floated by. Albert reached out, straining with all his might to touch it, but it was too far. It drifted away.

What had been elegant chairs, desks and tables were now just debris.

Paddle. Paddle.

He couldn't feel anything anymore. Not his feet. Not his hands. His fingers were getting stiffer, but he could still move them.

A broken dresser floated close by. He paddled

hard to get within reach of it. He touched the top, but his fingers slipped off. He paddled some more, then managed to get hold of a long, sharp edge. He curled his frozen fingers around it, then wrapped his arms around the sides of the dresser and drew it toward him.

Albert leaned his head against the dresser and took deep breaths. Then he lifted his head and peered around again. As he did, he felt something loosen around him. He touched his shoulder. His waist. His lifebelt was gone! There was nothing around him but his wet clothes.

Where was his lifebelt? He looked down. It had slipped off and was floating away. He reached out to grab it, but it was moving too fast. He'd need both arms to reach the lifebelt, but then he'd have to let go of the dresser.

Albert's heart sank as the lifebelt floated away. All he had now was the dresser. And the ship's stacks were about to fall.

CHAPTER NINE

With a thud the giant stacks smashed into the river, setting off huge waves and crushing a lifeboat filled with people. Their screams echoed through the night. Albert's heart thumped as he clung to the dresser. He shook from the force of the waves, but he held on. Salt water sprayed his face, stinging his eyes. He couldn't see. He could barely breathe.

Hold on. Hold on.

An explosion thundered through the river. Wood, glass and metal flew everywhere. People who had been clinging to the ship's port side were thrown into the water. The *Empress* was going under fast. And then she was gone. And so many were gone with her.

A wave of sadness and pain shot through Albert. Did his father make it? What about his uncle, aunt and Lewis? And Grace and her parents? Were they alive or . . . ?

Don't think about that, Albert told himself. *Just hold on.*

In the distance he saw a light. Was it a flare? And was something moving? A lifeboat? *Yes!* It wasn't far away. He lifted an icy hand and waved.

"Help! Here I am. Help!" he called. His voice was low and raspy. He called again. Louder this time. "Help me! Please!"

Did anyone see him? Hear him? He couldn't tell if the lifeboat was coming closer. It was so dark, it was hard to see anything clearly.

"Here! I'm alive. Please come!" he tried to shout louder. "Help!" He tried again and again, but the words sank into the river like the *Empress.*

The lifeboat wasn't moving toward him! It was moving away. They hadn't seen him at all.

Would anyone ever come? He scanned the river. All he could see were bodies. Fewer bodies than before.

It was quieter now in the water. He could only hear a few people calling for help, crying, sobbing, moaning. Albert knew what that meant. His tears mixed with salt water and stung his eyes again.

Don't cry. Not now.

He kept scanning the water for a ship or lifeboat. Someone had to see him. But it was so dark, and he was so weary. He leaned his head against the dresser. His eyes began to close.

No. No. Stay awake. He forced his eyes open. *You can't fall asleep. If you sleep, it will be over. Stay alert. Think about something. Do something. Anything.*

Albert began to sing. He sang "God Be with You," his mother's favourite hymn. He made up songs about his home on the farm in Ontario and walking up and down an English street with the Salvation Army band.

He pictured playing his trumpet again with the band. He imagined playing each note perfectly this time and his father beaming and shaking his hand. Albert had taken such care of his trumpet. He'd shined it up the night before the trip. But it was gone now. And his fellow musicians? Many of them were probably gone, too. But his father had to make it. He couldn't be . . .

No! Don't think about that, he told himself. *Not now. Think of something else.*

Albert pictured Grace sitting at the piano in the music room, her fingers positioned to play. He remembered her laughing. He pictured them standing together on the deck of the *Empress* that night. He remembered how they'd called that dark ship a ghost ship.

Soon after that everything had changed.

What had they hit? The ghost ship? It had been so close. Could the two ships have collided? But even if they had, how could *that* have destroyed the *Empress*? She was so solid. So strong. Everyone said so. But what else could have happened? What else could they have hit?

It was getting quieter and quieter around him. How much longer could he stay afloat? He was so cold, so achy, so tired. His eyes began to close again. It was as if they had a will of their own.

Don't sleep. You can't sleep. If you sleep, you might never wake up.

He forced his eyes open again. He looked out through the darkness.

Were his eyes playing tricks on him? Was that a boat in the distance? With his last ounce of energy he shouted, "I'm alive! Please come! Please help me!"

He lifted one arm off the dresser and waved. He waved again and again. Back and forth. Over and over. With the other arm he struggled to keep hold of the dresser.

No one waved back. No one heard him. Sadness and despair gripped him.

And then he saw movement. It was a small boat. A man was waving from a lifeboat!

Albert locked his eyes on the spot. A faint sound was coming from it.

"We're coming. Hold on." He could hear them now. He could see them now. There were several people in the lifeboat. Two of them were rowing. He only had to hold on until the lifeboat came.

"Hold on," called the voice. The lifeboat was drawing closer.

"We see you." The voices were clear now. The lifeboat stood out of the darkness like a light.

"Hurry! Please!" Albert called out. His teeth chattered. His arms felt as heavy as bricks. He didn't know how much longer he could cling to the dresser. If he let go, there was nothing else to keep him afloat.

Hold on. Hold on.

His fingers began to slide off the dresser.

CHAPTER TEN

Strong arms grabbed Albert. Two sailors hoisted him up into the lifeboat and wrapped him in blankets.

An older man sat across from him in the boat. His eyes were closed, but he was breathing. His black jacket was ripped. His white shirt was dirty and tattered. He had no shoes. The man opened his eyes for an instant. Pain streaked his face. "Dora," he mumbled. "Dora." Tears rolled down his cheeks. He closed his eyes again and groaned.

Albert looked down at his own feet. He had one shoe on. The other shoe and sock must have fallen off in the water. He touched his hair. It was matted and grimy.

Shivering, he nestled into the blankets. They were scratchy, but it didn't matter — they were dry and warm. He stroked the solid wood of the boat and leaned against it. His chest hurt when he breathed. His arms and legs were still numb with cold, but he was alive! He was out of the icy St. Lawrence. He was safe.

He thanked the two sailors over and over again. He told them his name. The sailor with a wide face, dimpled chin and sandy hair said that his name was Philip. He seemed to be in charge. The other sailor, Jan, was younger, with dark, stringy hair.

Philip patted Albert's arm. "Rest. No need to speak now."

Albert closed his eyes. All he felt was the rise and fall of the boat as it moved through the water. He drifted in and out of sleep.

❋   ❋   ❋

Albert woke with a jolt when the boat stopped. The sailors pulled in a young woman in a ripped nightgown. She had a dazed look in her eyes, and she kept murmuring, "My husband. Where is he?" She covered her face with her hands and sobbed.

Minutes later they rescued a young man in a life-belt. He was lean and tall with curly brown hair. His face was smeared with dirt and oil. His left eye and his lips were swollen. He sat back against the boat, breathing hard.

Albert rubbed his eyes. They still stung from the debris and salt in the water. It was hard to see clearly. Could it be?

"Lewis?" said Albert, stretching his hand out to the man. "It's me. Albert!"

The young man looked up at Albert. "I . . . I'm sorry. My name is Daniel, not Lewis. Is Lewis your brother?"

"Lewis is my cousin. You look a lot like him."

Daniel ran his fingers through his hair. "I hope your cousin is all right. I jumped just before the ship sank." Daniel coughed. "Sorry. It's hard to talk."

Daniel closed his eyes as the sailors rowed on. They peered out into the river and called again and again, "Anyone there? Call out if you're there. We've come to help."

But all they heard were oars slapping the water. They rowed on and on.

Then Philip called out, "Listen. I think I hear someone."

The sailors tried to locate the sounds. "Where are you?" they shouted.

"Here. Please. Help me," called a voice. The voice was hoarse and far away. "Please. Come quickly."

One of the sailors pointed. "I think that's where he is."

The sailors rowed hard. They kept calling, "Are we near you? Tell us if you can hear us."

"Hurry." The voice sounded fainter.

"Do you see him?" asked Philip.

"No," said Jan.

Philip and Jan called out over and over, but there was no reply.

"I fear he's gone," said Philip. He swallowed hard and looked down. "The water is awfully cold. It would be hard to last very long, even with a lifebelt."

His words sent a chill through Albert. If this lifeboat hadn't arrived when it had, he might be dead, too. He was rescued just in time.

CHAPTER ELEVEN

As the sailors rowed on, an eerie silence hung over the river. Albert closed his eyes. It was too painful to see more broken furniture and lifeless bodies float past.

Another lifeboat rowed up near them.

"Any luck? Did you find anyone?" called Philip.

"Just one woman this time. We found her clinging to a dead body. She's in terrible shape. We found more survivors the first time out. We're heading back to the ship. How about you?"

"We have four survivors with us. We found more people the first time out, too."

"What a nightmare. Stay safe, Philip. See you back at the *Storstad*."

"We'll take one more look around. I want to look one more time just in case . . . Then we'll join you."

"The *Storstad*?" said Albert. "What kind of ship is that?"

Philip took a deep breath. "It's a Norwegian collier. We carry coal."

"Were you close by when the *Empress* sank? Do you know what happened?"

Philip bit his lip.

"Please tell me what happened," said Albert.

Philip coughed. "We . . . we . . ." He cleared his throat. "The *Storstad* accidentally rammed into your ship. The fog was so dense . . . As soon as the accident happened, Captain Andersen ordered our lifeboats out to help. All our lifeboats have gone out several times. We've rescued some people but not as many as we'd hoped."

Suddenly the lifeboat stopped. A woman was floating nearby.

"She's wearing a lifebelt. I think I saw her move," shouted Jan. They rowed closer to the woman. Her eyes didn't blink. Her face was like a frozen mask. She was dead.

"Row back to the ship," said Philip. "It's time we returned."

Albert shivered and wrapped the scratchy wool blanket tighter around him. He tried to block out the look on the woman's face. Did she know she was dying? Did she die suddenly or lose consciousness and drift into an endless sleep?

What happened to his father, his family? What happened to Grace and her parents? Would anyone be alive?

CHAPTER TWELVE

Albert stared at the *Storstad*. It didn't look like a ghost ship now. It was a hard-working, gritty vessel that had dealt the *Empress* a death blow.

He watched as the three other survivors from the *Empress* were helped off the lifeboat. Daniel moaned with each step as he made his way slowly up the shaky rope ladder.

"My husband. I must find him," sobbed the young woman. She trembled as she climbed the swaying ladder.

The old man's glassy eyes stared ahead as he climbed. He kept staring as the ship's crewmembers helped him on deck.

It was Albert's turn to step off the lifeboat. He was

dizzy when he stood up. He almost fell backwards, but Philip grabbed him and helped him regain his balance. Albert's legs shook on the rope ladder. He held the rough rope tightly so he wouldn't slip.

The deck of the *Storstad* overflowed with people. Some survivors huddled in a corner drinking hot tea or coffee. Many were wrapped in blankets. Others wore ill-fitting clothes the *Storstad* crew had provided. Some were wrapped in curtains, while others covered themselves with canvas sacks. The survivors had been given whatever clothing was available.

The old man from the lifeboat tapped a sailor on the arm. "Have you seen Dora Smith?" he asked.

"No. Sorry. Ask around," said the sailor.

The old man repeated the question to the next sailor. When his response was no, too, he tapped on the arm of a woman wrapped in a blanket.

"I am so sorry, but no," she said.

The old man asked person after person about his wife. With each no, his eyes grew sadder, heavier, more distant.

Albert walked around the deck looking at faces, peering into corners, desperate to find his family.

Albert didn't see anyone from the Salvation Army.

"Here, put this on. Get out of those wet clothes," said Philip. He held out a pair of pants and a shirt.

"Whose are these?" asked Albert.

"They're mine. They may be a bit big for you, but they're clean and warm. Go on. Put them on."

Albert nodded and followed Philip into a corridor off the deck. No one was around as Albert slipped into the clothes. Philip was right. The clothes were too big. The pants hung down and dragged on the floor. The sleeves dangled over Albert's hands. But it felt good to be wearing something dry and warm.

"Thanks," said Albert. He smiled for the first time since the *Empress* was hit. "How do I look?"

"A bit like a clown. But don't worry," said Philip, smiling back, "you can roll the sleeves and the legs up. We can't have you tripping and breaking a leg. Are you still dizzy?"

"I'm better, but I have to get used to walking

around on a ship again, especially in oversized clothes."

Albert imagined what Grace would say if she could see him now. She'd tell him that the rest of his clothes matched his big Stetson hat.

It felt like a week since he and Grace had stood in line together waiting to board the *Empress*. It felt like a week since he'd first seen the ghost ship approach. It felt like a week since they'd gazed out at the calm river in the early hours of the morning, commenting on the sudden appearance of fog.

But it wasn't a ghost ship. It was the *Storstad*. It wasn't a week. It was only a few hours ago. In those few hours Albert's whole life had changed. He wasn't going to England. The band would never perform there. His uniform was gone. His hat was at the bottom of the sea with his trumpet. So many people he knew were probably gone, too.

Albert rolled up the legs and the sleeves of Philip's clothes. "Thanks for the clean clothes. I wish I could take a bath and wash up."

"You will. Soon. We're heading for shore."

"Do you know if there's a list of survivors?"

"I think a list is being put together now. It will take some time. Some people were picked up by other vessels. We should know more when we reach land. Who were you travelling with, Albert?"

"My father, my uncle, my aunt and my cousin Lewis. We were travelling with the Salvation Army. How do I let my mother and brother back home know that I'm all right?"

"They'll start notifying family as quickly as they can. Try not to think too much about any of that now. Think about getting stronger. You've been through a lot."

"But I have to know what's happened to my family. I have to know what happened to Grace O'Riley and her parents, too. We were together on the deck. Then we jumped."

"I'll start asking around, but don't despair if you

don't know anything immediately. The *Storstad* only picked up some of the survivors. I'm sure there are many more, picked up by other vessels. The *Lady Evelyn* and the *Eureka* sailed out as soon as they were aware of the collision."

Philip was trying to be hopeful, but Albert couldn't help wondering how many people could have survived such a powerful impact. How many people could have made it off the ship before it slid into the river? It had happened so quickly. There was little time to react.

CHAPTER THIRTEEN

"There are some people down below in the boiler rooms," said Philip. "Perhaps there's someone down there you know. Come on. I'll go down with you."

Albert and Philip headed down the stairs.

It was hot and crowded in the boiler room. The air was thick, and it was hard to breathe. Albert coughed so hard he almost gagged. The light from the furnaces and greasy lamps stung his eyes.

The room was jammed with people milling about, rubbing their hands to warm up and drying their wet clothes. Some passengers, too weak and injured to stand alone, leaned against others. Many looked dazed. Others grimaced in pain.

Some cried as if they couldn't stop. Some called out names. One woman kept repeating, "Why?" over and over. One man cursed.

There were no children in the room. The realization made Albert shudder and tears well up in his eyes. There had been almost 150 children aboard the *Empress*. He'd heard that at dinner. Had they all died except him?

And where were all the Salvation Army people? There was no one he knew here. Someone from the Salvation Army had to be alive. He couldn't be the only survivor. But what if he was? He couldn't let himself think about that. It hurt too much.

"Please, can we go back up?" he asked Philip.

Philip patted his arm. "Of course."

They walked back up to the deck.

Albert gripped the railing and exhaled.

"You need something to warm you up. How about some hot soup?"

"All right. Thank you."

"Wait here. I'll bring it to you."

As Albert waited, he sat down on the hard deck. A man sat beside him, with his back to Albert. There was something familiar about him. The man turned and leaned against the railing. Albert couldn't believe it! It was Captain Kendall, the captain of the *Empress*! Albert remembered how the captain had toured the deck in his crisp uniform, meeting passengers, shaking hands, wishing them all a good journey when they boarded the ship. Now his uniform was dirty, ragged and torn.

He sat with his face in his palms. When he looked up, his eyes were glazed, like he'd seen a ghost.

Dr. Grant, the *Empress*'s doctor, approached the captain. Albert recognized him from the ship, too. The doctor had listened to them play on deck. He'd shaken hands with everyone in the band.

"Here. Have some brandy," the doctor told the captain, handing him a dusty bottle. "It will warm you up."

The captain looked up and shook his head. "I never drink liquor, doctor, and I can't now. Thank you anyway."

"You shouldn't have stayed out so long looking for survivors. You're hurt and exhausted, Henry."

"I had to go. They are my passengers. The *Empress* was my ship. She was my responsibility. Why didn't the *Storstad* stop? I signalled her. All this would have been avoided if she'd stopped."

"I am so sorry this has happened," said the doctor. "The fog was thick. It was hard to see anything through it."

Captain Kendall shook his head. He looked out over the water. "Look. The *Lady Evelyn* is approaching. She'll be transporting survivors to Rimouski. From there, they'll make their way home. You go on ahead, doctor. You're needed. We couldn't have managed without you."

The doctor patted the captain on the back and hurried off to assist in moving passengers to the

Lady Evelyn. Soon after, the captain stood up, pulled back his shoulders and walked over to help the doctor.

Albert looked up as the *Lady Evelyn* drew closer. Soon he'd be heading home.

Home. It seemed so far away and yet he'd been home only a few days ago.

Philip brought hot soup, brown bread and a cup of water. Albert sipped the soup. It was thin, almost a broth, with a few onions and potatoes floating around, but it tasted good. Albert hadn't realized how hungry he was until then.

As he ate, he watched the *Lady Evelyn* stop beside the *Storstad*. He watched Dr. Grant direct the transfer of the living and dead. Albert looked away as the dead were brought out. Someone he knew might be among them. He put down his soup bowl and waited for the sad procession to end.

Next the severely injured were carried aboard. Those who could walk would follow. Albert stood up. He handed Philip the empty bowl and cup.

Philip put his arm around Albert's shoulder. "You are a brave boy, Albert. I hope you find your family and your friend. Don't give up hope. You made it. They could have made it, too."

"Thank you again for rescuing me. Thank you for everything."

Albert waved to Philip as he joined the other survivors aboard the *Lady Evelyn*.

CHAPTER FOURTEEN

Albert looked around the crowded *Lady Evelyn*. That ship was usually loaded with mail. It transported letters and postcards from the cruise liners to the train in Rimouski, where they were carried on to cities and towns around the world.

The steward on the *Empress* had promised to post Albert's card to his mother and Eddie so it could be picked up by the *Lady Evelyn*.

And here he was on that very same mail ship. But now it had picked up the dead, the injured, the survivors of the *Empress* instead of letters and postcards.

Albert's stomach tightened. How awful to receive a letter from someone who died just hours after it was written. When Albert wrote his card he was excited about the trip across the Atlantic. He couldn't wait to reach England and watch the Salvation Army band perform. And now . . . now he was on his way home.

He had to find his father. His father had to be alive. How could his mother and brother cope without him? How could he? And what about his uncle, aunt and cousin? His cousin was young. And though Albert hated it when Lewis treated him like a little kid, he wished he could hear Lewis call him "kid" again.

Albert closed his eyes. *Remember what Philip said. You made it. They might have, too.*

Albert scanned the faces of the people on the deck. As they'd boarded the *Lady Evelyn*, he'd spotted a young man of about twenty that he recognized from the Salvation Army. He was limping. It looked like he'd injured his leg. Albert didn't know his name, but he'd seen him back in Toronto when they'd boarded the train for Quebec City at Union Station. Where was that man now? Maybe he knew something about the others from the Salvation Army.

Albert peered over the railing. They were nearing Rimouski. He could see the pier.

"Good. Land!" said a man beside him. He had a thick Irish accent. "That's it for me with the sea. I've been lucky two times. I won't chance a third."

"You've been lucky two times?" said Albert.

"You've heard of the *Titanic*, haven't you, lad?" said the man.

"Of course."

"Well, I was on that ship. I was a stoker there, too. Worked the furnaces on both vessels. William Clark's the name." He stretched out his hand to Albert.

"I'm Albert McBride." Albert couldn't believe someone had survived two disasters at sea in just over two years. "You took another job at sea on the *Empress*?"

"I liked the *Empress*. She was sturdy. Maybe not as fancy as the *Titanic* but solid and well built. She'd plied the Atlantic waters many times. What could go wrong?"

"The fog. I saw it come in while I was on deck with a friend."

"Where is your friend now?"

"I don't know. She jumped from the deck like me."

The man raised his eyebrows. "A young lady? I hope she made it."

"She knows how to swim, and she was wearing a lifebelt."

"Then she stands a good chance." William patted Albert on the shoulder. "Take courage, whatever happens. You're a survivor, like me."

Albert held on to the railing as the ship slowed down. His legs felt weak. They were pulling into the pier at Rimouski. It would be strange to step on land after all these hours. What would he learn when he reached the town? How would he get home from there?

"I wish you the best of luck, Albert," said William Clark. "May your luck continue."

"I hope your luck continues, too," said Albert.

CHAPTER FIFTEEN

Rimouski was bedlam. Although it was early morning, crowds greeted the ship when it docked. Newspapermen and photographers jammed the pier. All the townspeople seemed to be out, waiting for the survivors. Everyone was talking about the *Empress*. They wanted to know how such a tragedy could happen. They wanted to help.

The crowd watched solemnly as the bodies were taken off the ship. They watched as the injured were carried off on stretchers, and doctors and nurses from all around rushed over to help. They watched as the survivors stumbled off the boat. Many were still dazed, startled by the noise and the crowds.

Albert knew they were a sad-looking group, but all he could think about was finding his family and Grace.

Comments and rumours swirled around as Albert and the other survivors made their way down the pier. Newspaper reporters and photographers asked questions, snapped pictures.

"Did you hear Captain Kendall was drunk?"

"No. I hear he never drinks."

"I heard that the ship wasn't built properly."

"Nonsense. She was a strong ship."

"I heard that many of the crew survived. Why didn't they rescue more passengers?"

"Look at those poor people. They're in rags," said a woman clutching a bag of clothes. "I'm glad I brought these. All my neighbours pitched in to donate."

"Imagine! Those poor people were in the water in the middle of the night," said an older man with a cane. "I don't know how anyone made it through."

"This way. This way," said a sailor from the *Lady Evelyn*. "Follow me. We'll get you all clean clothes and food."

Albert followed the line of survivors to a brick building. As soon as he entered, volunteers rushed over, handing out clean clothing, cups of strong tea, fresh bread and hot soup.

"Do you know if anyone from the Salvation Army is here?" Albert asked a woman with curly white hair and a warm smile.

"I think I heard of a Salvation Army lad, older than you, who just came in. He was asking for news of his family and others in your group." The woman pointed. "Over there."

Albert's stomach knotted. Could it be Lewis? He didn't want to get his hopes dashed again.

Albert thanked the woman and hurried over to where she had pointed. His heart was thumping hard against his chest.

A young man was standing behind a curtain

held up by a woman. Albert could only see the top of his head. His hair was brown and curly like Lewis's. There was a gash across his forehead.

"Excuse me," said Albert. "I'm looking for—"

Before Albert could finish his sentence, the young man popped out from behind the curtain. He only had a pair of pants on, and his right arm was in a sling.

"Albert!" he shouted. He tossed his left arm around Albert's neck. He smelled of the river and his hair was dirty, but it was Lewis! Albert couldn't believe it.

"It's you. It's really you. You're alive!" Albert said.

"I am, kid," he said, jabbing Albert in the arm with his left hand.

"What happened to you? To Father, Uncle Thomas and Aunt Betsy?"

Lewis's face clouded over. "My dad is gone, Albert. I saw him get sucked under the ship when she went down."

"Oh, Lewis."

Lewis bit his lip. Tears dribbled down his cheeks.

Albert put his arm around Lewis's shoulder. "Uncle Thomas insisted I hurry on deck and not wait for anything."

"I know. He rushed me out of the cabin. My life-belt was tangled, and he fixed it and made me put it on before he put his on."

"Did you reach the boat deck?"

"Just in time. But we wouldn't have made it there if you hadn't come for us. You saved my life, Albert."

"We were lucky that our cabins were not on the starboard side of the ship. None of us would have made it if they were."

Lewis nodded. "I know. The ship was sinking fast when we reached the deck. There was no time left to do anything. There were no lifeboats around, so we jumped. I saw Father go down and disappear under the ship. I made it clear of the *Empress* just in time. The *Eureka* picked me up a little while later."

"And Aunt Betsy?"

"She jumped, too. I saw her in the water. I heard her scream when Father got sucked under, but I didn't see her after that. I'm afraid she didn't make it either. I can't stop thinking about my parents. And your father, Albert? Do you have any news?"

Albert shook his head. "Father was going to jump after me. I don't know what happened to him."

Lewis hugged his cousin. "It's too much to take in. Our family . . . All those people we knew." Lewis sobbed. "Sorry, Albert. I never cry. I just feel . . . it's just too much. How could this happen, Albert? How?"

CHAPTER SIXTEEN

It was hard to say anything. A lump stuck in Albert's throat. All he could do was shake his head over and over. How could his uncle, his aunt and his father be gone forever? *It can't be true!* he wanted to shout.

He couldn't stop thinking about his father and aunt. What if they were hurt? Where would they be? Was anyone helping them?

And what should he and Lewis do next? Some people were going to the boatshed. That's where they were keeping bodies until they could be identified.

"Were you going to the boatshed to see . . . about Aunt Betsy?" Albert asked Lewis.

"I don't want to. Just the thought of it makes me

feel sick. But I have to go. I'll look for your father too, Albert."

"Thank you, Lewis. I . . . I . . . can't stop thinking about them. I can't stop wondering what happened."

"Me, too." Lewis patted Albert's back. "Wait for me here. I'll come back as soon as I can. This may be harder than hitting that icy river."

Lewis squeezed Albert's shoulder and walked out the door of the building. Albert sat down on a bench.

In a few minutes Lewis was back. His face was white, and he was shaking.

"I walked over to the boatshed and opened the door, but I couldn't go in. I don't know what to do, Albert."

"I'll go with you," said Albert.

"You can't. You're just a kid."

"I'm not a kid, Lewis. Not anymore."

Lewis rubbed his hand across his forehead. "You're right. But are you sure you want to do this?"

"I'm sure."

Albert's stomach knotted as he and his cousin walked toward the boatshed. He didn't want to go in, but he had to. For a minute the cousins stood beside the entrance to the boatshed. Then Lewis took a deep breath, pushed the door open and stepped in. Albert followed.

Silently the boys joined a line of surviors walking up and down the rows of makeshift wooden coffins, glancing at each body as they passed. Halfway through the boatshed, Lewis grabbed Albert's hand.

"Oh no! That's Simon," said Lewis. "He was one of my father's friends. I can't look."

"Don't look. There's nothing we can do."

The cousins walked on. The only sounds were the occasional wails and screams of people spotting a family member who'd died.

"Mary!"

"Father!"

"Lizzy!"

It was horrible to hear the anguished cries. Albert knew that at any moment he might see someone he knew. Someone he loved.

Albert swallowed hard, trying to make the sour taste that kept rising in his throat go away. But the bad taste kept getting stronger. *Only a few more steps and you'll be out of the boatshed*, he told himself.

Beside him, Lewis groaned. Sweat poured down his face. And then, just as they were close to the door leading out, Lewis touched Albert's shoulder. "No. I think it's . . ."

Albert looked down. The woman in the box resembled Lewis's mother. "It's not Aunt Betsy, Lewis."

"I see that now." Lewis quickly pushed the door leading out of the boatshed.

"I . . . I . . ." he muttered. He raced ahead. Albert ran after him. He reached him just as Lewis leaned against a wall and threw up. "Sorry. I feel like I'm the kid now."

"It's okay," said Albert. "It was horrible in there. I thought I'd be sick the whole time. Come on. Let's go back to the building."

As soon as they entered the brick building, a woman in a blue-checkered apron over a blue-and-white dress approached them with soup and bread. Her grey hair was in a bun.

"Have some chicken soup," she offered. "You both look like you need it."

"Thank you," said Albert. "We've been . . . in the boatshed."

"That must have been awful. Did you . . ."

"No. There's no one from our family in there. Thank you for asking. Thank you for your kindness."

"It could have been any of us on that ship. All of us want to help."

Albert sipped the soup slowly.

"Here, young man." The woman handed Lewis a bowl of soup, too.

"Thanks," said Lewis, pushing a curl out of his

eyes. "This looks just like my mother's soup."

"What's your mother's name?" she asked.

"Betsy McBride."

"Does she have hair like yours?"

"Yes."

"There's a woman that was just brought in. She's in shock. She kept saying the name Thomas. Is that you?"

Lewis's eyes lit up. He put down the bowl. "Thomas is my father's name. Where is she?"

"I'll show you."

Albert and Lewis followed the woman to the other end of the building. A woman with curly, brown hair and wearing a brown dress two sizes too big for her was sitting on a bench. She was staring ahead. Tears rolled down her cheeks.

"Mother!" cried Lewis. "It's me!"

Lewis's mother turned. Her eyes grew wide. She grabbed her son's hand. She held it tightly. "Lewis? Lewis? Is that really you? Your father . . ."

"I know, Mother. I'm so happy we found you. And look, Albert is here, too."

She grasped Albert's hand. "I can't believe you're both here. I was sure I had lost you. I looked everywhere. I asked everyone I saw. Then I thought . . . the worst. But you're alive — both of you."

CHAPTER SEVENTEEN

The journey back to Quebec City the next day was quiet and sombre. Albert glanced at the other passengers on the special train transporting them from Rimouski. Many were still in shock. Many spoke in whispers, remembering the people they had lost. Most still could not believe how quickly their lives had changed.

Albert thought about his father, his uncle, Grace and her parents. Only his uncle's name was on a list of the dead posted before they left Rimouski, but the lists were incomplete. It was unlikely Grace had made it out alive — so few children had survived. So far it looked like only three had lived through the collision. And few of their large Salvation Army group had made it.

A crowd greeted the train at the station in Quebec City. So many people had gathered that it was hard to get through to the waiting cars. The survivors who were not badly injured, like Albert, Lewis and Aunt Betsy, were taken to the Château Frontenac.

It was a beautiful building. It looked like a castle in a fairy tale.

"I wish my Thomas were here to see this," said Aunt Betsy when they arrived. "Life will never be the same without him."

"I'll help you, Mother," said Lewis. "We'll manage together."

"I know, dear. And that does help. More than you know. And it helps to have you here with me here too, Albert. Lewis and I wouldn't be here if it weren't for you."

"We were lucky," said Albert.

"I just wish Thomas and your father were with us." Tears sprang to his aunt's eyes.

Albert hugged his aunt. He couldn't stop thinking about his uncle and father. How could he face Eddie and his mother? What would he say to them?

Albert stared out the window of the hotel room. It felt unreal staying in such an elegant hotel after all that had happened.

There was a knock at the door. Lewis hurried to answer it.

"Albert! Come quick!" he called.

Albert turned around. He stared at the man standing in the doorway.

"Albert." The man's voice was shaky and hoarse. A large bandage covered his head. His nose was swollen. His arm was in a sling, and he limped as he took a step forward.

"Father!" Albert shouted. He ran over and wrapped his arms around his father. "You're alive! I was sure you were . . . Oh, Father."

"I thought I was gone, too, Albert. I didn't know where or who I was when I woke up in the hospital."

"I can't believe you're here. I'm so happy to see you. I . . . I . . ."

"I know, son."

"Uncle Thomas . . ."

"Yes. I heard just before I came up." Albert's father held back tears. "I will miss him more than I can say."

* * *

Albert, his father, Lewis and his aunt returned to Toronto on the train the next day. So did the coffins. When they arrived at Union Station, crowds met the train. The draped coffins were carried in a solemn procession through Toronto.

A week later, a church service was held with many in the city paying their respects to those who had perished on the *Empress of Ireland*.

At the church, people kept coming over to shake Albert's hand and to tell him how much they had admired his uncle, and how glad they were that Albert, his father, his aunt and his cousin had survived. He still couldn't believe what had happened to them. Only a week ago they'd boarded the *Empress*, and now he was part of a funeral procession winding its way slowly to the Mount Pleasant Cemetery. Albert played the trumpet beside his father and Lewis. Their new bandmaster had insisted. Albert was the youngest member of the Salvation Army band that day.

His mother and Eddie watched the procession, but Aunt Betsy stayed home. They'd never found Uncle Thomas's body, and she said she couldn't bear to attend the services.

After the service at the cemetery, Albert and his family stood beside the graves. Albert remembered his uncle and how kind he had always been to him. He remembered how excited they all were about the trip to England and how they'd talked about what they were going to do there as they rode on the train from Toronto to Quebec City. He remembered standing in line waiting to board the ship and meeting Grace. The list of the dead and missing was still incomplete.

"Albert?"

Albert looked up. His eyes widened. He gasped.

"It's me. Grace."

The girl standing in front of him looked different from a few days ago; her eyes had lost their sparkle. "I . . . I . . . thought you were . . ."

"Dead. I know. Father and I had to stay in Quebec. We were too sick to travel. We only came home yesterday."

"And your mother?"

Grace bit her lip. "Mother . . . didn't make it."

"I'm sorry."

"I miss her terribly but . . . it helped to hear you play again, Albert. I saw you march in the procession. You never missed a note. You played perfectly."

Albert smiled. Grace was right.

It felt good to play the trumpet again and honour all the people he'd known who were gone.

It felt good to march proudly beside his father and Lewis.

It felt good to hear his father say, "Well done, son. Well done."

Author's Note

Say the word *"Titanic"* and everyone knows something about that ill-fated ship that sank off the coast of Newfoundland over a hundred years ago. Countless books have been written about every aspect of that tragedy. Blockbuster movies have brought the story to life.

But *Titanic* wasn't the only great ocean liner to suffer a terrible fate in the early twentieth century. On May 29, 1914, a little after two a.m., the *Empress of Ireland* — a large, elegant ship that regularly sailed between Canada and England — sank in the St. Lawrence River after being accidentally rammed by the coal-bearing ship *Storstad*. More passengers died on the *Empress* (840) than on the *Titanic* (829), and yet for a long time the *Empress of Ireland* was almost forgotten.

Why was so little known about the *Empress* for so many years? Many believe that at the time the *Empress* sank, world attention was drawn to the battlefields of Europe and the increasingly grim news from World War I. There was much less interest in a non-war-related tragedy like the sinking of the *Empress*.

But in 2014 that changed. It was the 100th anniversary of the tragedy, and that milestone sparked renewed interest in the *Empress*, its passengers and the events of that terrible night. There were museum exhibits, stamps, coins and memorial services. Many people wondered what was left of the ship lying at the bottom of the St. Lawrence River.

There were also ceremonies honouring the ship and its passengers, especially in Quebec and Ontario. For years the Salvation Army

A postcard of the Empress of Ireland from 1909

had commemorated the sinking of the *Empress* because so many of its members were lost in the tragedy. One hundred and sixty-seven Salvation Army members boarded the ship, bound for a large convention in London, England. About forty were part of the Salvation Army band. They were a lively, friendly group, and they helped create a festive atmosphere onboard. They even played on deck just as the ship was leaving Quebec City.

Everything changed, of course, when the *Storstad* and the *Empress* collided. Many people drowned or were fatally injured by falling debris from the

The collier *Storstad* after the collision

ship, including 128 members of the Salvation Army. Many of the senior leaders of the organization, and most members of the band, perished.

Shipwreck! is a fictional account of the sinking of the *Empress*. I based my main character, Albert McBride, on members of the Salvation Army. Albert's friend, Grace O'Riley, is inspired by Helen O'Hara — a ten-year-old passenger who knew how to swim, a skill that helped her survive in the icy river. The other characters are made up, except Captain Kendall, Captain Andersen, Dr. Grant and William Clark.

~Frieda Wishinsky

Facts About the
Empress of Ireland

- About 120,000 immigrants to Canada sailed on the *Empress of Ireland* from the day she was first launched in January 1906. Estimates are that about a million Canadians are descended from those immigrants.

- The passengers on the *Empress's* fatal last journey on May 28, 1914, came from many countries, including Japan, New Zealand, Fiji, England, the United States and Canada.

- There were some celebrities on that last voyage. Laurence Irving and his wife Mabel Hackney were great stage actors. Big-game hunter Sir Henry Seton-Karr was aboard, as was author Ella Hart Bennett. They all died in the accident.

- The black-painted collier, the *Storstad*, was a

Norwegian ship carrying Cape Breton coal.

- The *Empress* sank in the St. Lawrence River nine hours and forty-three minutes after she left Quebec City.

- Historians believe there are two reasons the *Empress* sank: She was sliced deep into the starboard side of the ship below the water-line, and the airtight doors and portholes weren't completely closed, even though maritime regulations state that all portholes had to be closed and locked before a ship leaves port.

- It took a while to determine who had died and who had survived the tragedy because there was confusion about names on the passenger list.

- Only 4 out of the 138 children aboard the ship survived.

- Only 41 out of the 310 women aboard the ship survived.

- Only 172 out of 609 men aboard survived.

- 248 members of the crew survived. There were 420 crew members originally on board.

- When the *Empress* sank, Captain Kendall was thrown from the bridge into the water. He swam to the surface and clung to a wooden grate until a lifeboat picked him up.

- Many consider Dr. Grant a hero in the disaster. He saved many lives and helped calm people who were injured and distressed. McGill University later presented him with a duplicate diploma to replace the one he lost on the *Empress*.

- There was a Canadian commission of inquiry into the accident. It started on May 30, 1914 and lasted for eleven days. The conclusion of the inquiry was that the collision was the fault of Captain Andersen of the *Storstad* for changing course in the fog. A Norwegian commission blamed Captain Kendall.

- Half a dozen divers have died investigating the wreckage of the *Empress*. Although the wreckage lies not far from shore, in the St. Lawrence River and is accessible to divers, strong currents, poor visibility, cold water and under-water objects, such as wires, make diving difficult and dangerous.

- Canada has designated the site as a historic landmark to preserve what remains of the ship and to discourage further diving and the removal of objects from the wreckage.

ALSO AVAILABLE

ISBN 978-1-4431-4638-8

In a matter of seconds, Alex's world is turned upside down. What started out as the perfect day to build an epic snow fort turns into his worst nightmare. Injured and disoriented, can Alex find his classmates trapped in the deadly snow?